P9-DCP-574

HELLO, SPRING!

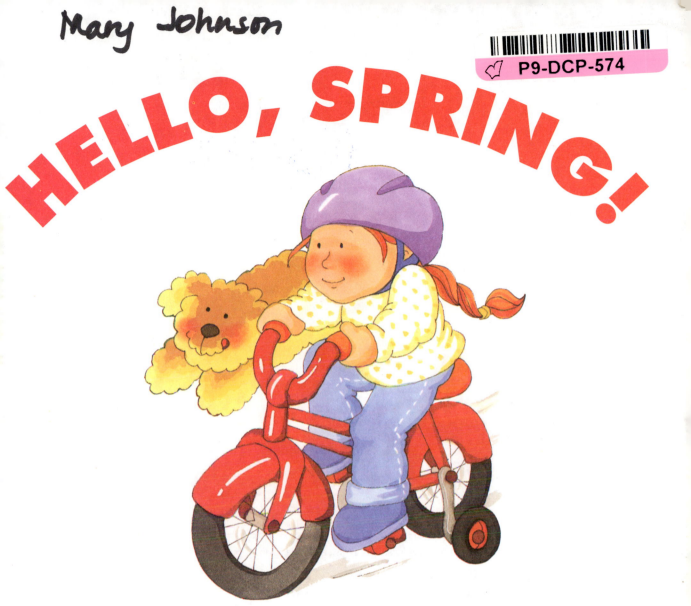

by Mary Packard
Illustrated by Jill Dubin

SCHOLASTIC INC.

New York   Toronto   London   Auckland   Sydney

Cartwheel
B·O·O·K·S®

To Henry and Nina with love.
—J.D.

Text copyright © 1998 by Mary Packard.
Illustrations copyright © 1998 by Jill Dubin.
All rights reserved. Published by Scholastic Inc.
CARTWHEEL BOOKS and the CARTWHEEL BOOKS logo
are trademarks and/or registered trademarks of Scholastic Inc.

ISBN 0-590-11508-1

10 9 8 7 6 5 4 3 2 1   8 9/9 0/0 01 02

Printed in the U.S.A.   24
First printing, March 1998

**Good-bye, winter.
Hello, spring!**

Good-bye, jacket.

Hello, swing!

Hello, skates.

Hello, bike.

It's time to play

the games we like.

Hello, ducklings.

Go ahead!

So many babies

must be fed!

Bunnies hop

and robins sing.

Hello, sunshine.
Hello, spring!